MW00681966

Cover Me

Mariko Tamaki

McGilligan Books

Canadian Cataloguing in Publication Data

Tamaki, Mariko
  Cover me
ISBN 0-9698064-9-3
I. Title.
PS8589.A768C68 2000   C813'.6   C00-932190-X
PR9199.3.T33C68 2000

copyright © Mariko Tamaki 2000
Editor: Ann Decter
Copy editor: Noreen Shanahan
Layout: Heather Guylar
Interior Illustrations: Kathryn Boyd
Cover Photo: Sophie Hackett
Cover Design: Heather Guylar

"Lords of the Dance" lyrics from the hymn "Lord of the Dance" by Sydney Carter 1963 Stainer & Bell Ltd. (Admin. Hope Publishing Co., Carol Stream, IL 60188). All rights reserved. Used by permission.

All rights reserved. No part of this book may be reproduced in any manner whatsoever without written permission, except in the case of brief quotations in critical articles or reviews. For information contact McGilligan Books, P.O. Box 16024, 859 Dundas Street West, Toronto, ON, Canada, M6J 1W0, ph (416)538-0945, e-mail mcgilbks@idirect.com.

We acknowledge the support of the Canada Council for the Arts for our publishing program.

The Canada Council | Le Conseil des Arts
for the Arts | du Canada

ONTARIO ARTS
COUNCIL

CONSEIL DES ARTS
DE L'ONTARIO

Acknowledgements

Cover Me is dedicated to my family, my benevolent benefactors, who are the reason I'm still here.

Thanks to my friends and my therapist, who are the reason I'm still sane.

Special thanks to Ann Decter, editor, mentor, and rock star, who made this book happen.

This book is fiction,
which means it's only as true as it needs to be.

Epiphanies

If my mother was in charge, the story of my life would begin the day she first conceived of me, staring into the window of the Three Little Bears, a shoe shop on Yonge Street. She was twenty-four years old, married, and shopping for a practical winter jacket, something every Canadian woman must have, when she spotted a pair of tiny white shoes in the window.

Tiny white girl shoes for tiny white stocking feet.

My mother says that was when she first realized she was going to have a little girl. She wasn't even pregnant. It was a Window Shopping Epiphany. She looked in the window, through the glass, and saw my little body sprouting up and out from tiny white shoes.

7

My mother was not a big fan of premonitions. She was a big fan of those shoes. When I tell this story, I say my mother was dressing me before I was born.

It says a lot about parenting. About our parents knitting us bodies and buying us shoes before we even step into the world.

Since this is my story, and not my mother's, my life begins the day I was born, near the middle of December. A snowstorm so thick Mom thought she would have me in the car on the side of the road. She didn't. I was born in a hospital, pulled out with forceps when, halfway through the delivery, I tilted my head up and got stuck.

The forceps dented my head temporarily, shaping the tender skull enough so when my father first saw me I looked like a Coke bottle.

An ugly little crying Coke bottle, he said, *on Christmas*.

You were a strange little kid then, he told me recently, and you're a strange kid now.

I'm twenty. It's 1996.

Who cares?

In the Beginning, There was Lunch

I emerge, out of breath, from the toothless mouth of the cool musky subway station, and walk briskly, bangles pumping on my wrists in the clammy palm of early summer heat. It's Thursday afternoon and I'm downtown to meet my dad for lunch.

"12:15 p.m. Sharp."

It's very Father, very Toronto, to meet someone on a time with "sharp" point on the end. We have arranged this meeting over a series of answering machine messages, each message shorter and shorter as my father squeezed what he sees as my impossibly messy schedule into his grid-map social calendar. "Sharp."

Twenty-four hours ago I didn't even own a watch (I do now – thanks to the small variety store next to our hotel), something my father would know. Somewhere in the deep dark corners of this city lie all the lost watches my father ever bought me.

"Something in this city likes to eat watches," I once told him.

"Someone in this city likes to lose them," he answered. "Watches don't grow on trees you know."

"No, they grow in malls."

My new ten dollar sports watch, still stiff and smelling like packaging, informs me I have exactly eleven minutes and forty-four seconds before I have to go inside.

Good to know.

12:05 p.m. I light a smoke even though I know he'll smell it on me. My father finally ceased to comment on my smoking, not that he ever exactly protested. There was a period in my teens when my friends and I would sneak out for smokes at night.

"We're going for a walk," I'd call, with the impudence of a fifteen-year-old who thinks she knows something her parents don't, an illusion that shattered one night when my friend Lucy and I got half way around the block to find my dad swinging on the swing in the park.

"What are you doing here!" I screamed, incensed.

"I'm going for a walk too," my dad replied, continuing to swing. "Hey, you guys wouldn't happen to have a *cigarette* on you, would you?"

For the past twenty-five years my father has worked in one of those skyscrapers in the concrete forest of the Toronto business district. Penis country, my friend calls it, because of the plethora of phallic symbols and suits. King Street, a Mecca of concrete con- trasted by a few, small, ill-looking, token trees in little grey corpo- rate cubicles. It's a land without pity, sucking the life out through the souls of my shoes as I puff thoughtfully on my cigarette and survey the secretaries in their business suits and Nikes, basking like seals in the sun. Modern seals, with protein drinks and outrageous Visa bills.

12:08 p.m. I pause to write a song lyric about how I will never sell-out and wear Nikes and nylons.

12:09 p.m. What rhymes with sell-out?

12:10 p.m. A group of hungry looking Goths is selling wilted pansies from a bucket. "Satan's Stems two dollars." I hear secretaries conspiring to call the cops and have them "removed."

"Hey," I call out, making a quick detour in their direction before heading indoors, "You'd better leave."

It takes me a while to explain King Street is not a Satan's Stems kind of district.

"Man," says the smaller Goth in an old ratty black lace skirt and white silk shirt, "this sucks. Toronto is so uptight."

"Where are you from?" I ask.

"Vancouver."

"Try Queen Street," I suggest, "if that doesn't work, try Montreal."

A tall girl with spiked hair and heavy eyeliner twirling around her left eye is apparently in charge; she nods silently. They pick up their buckets and head towards the sidewalk.

"Thanks."

Secretaries disturb as easily as a flock of pigeons. By the time I turn around, they have taken flight. Creepy.

12:13 p.m. I extinguish my cigarette and push through the thick slabs of heavy glass that serve as doors. It requires all my strength to wedge them open. I'm sure there's an entrance with normal doors. These doors are probably just here to intimidate people like me and make clients feel important.

Mission accomplished.

Inside, the air smells of money and lemon polish. Huge murals composed of rough metal spikes banged into heavy marble walls keep watch as I pad my way to the main reception desk. The little electronic eyes of a million security cameras focus on the small of my back. My skin is already itching as I lean on the marble counter and ask to be buzzed in. The receptionist, tall and pointy behind her little perch of power, frowns at my purple hair and raises an eyebrow.

Yes, I reassure her in a brief psychic message, I am your nightmare. One day your children will look like me.

"He works for Cameron and Stewart," I say, "can't you look him up? It's Miki Yamoto."

"With two m's?"

"Actually it's five m's but four of them are silent."

"I beg your pardon?"

"One m. YA-MO-TO."

Glancing down at her monitor the receptionist frowns as she scans the screen.

Tick, tick, tick.

"Like the car," she finally says.

I have this theory that all receptionists have to take a course that teaches them to make their job seem harder and more important than it really is.

"Yeah, like the *car*. Hey, that's a new one."

I try not to squirm amid the polite coughs and tapping of expensive Italian soles on the polished floor as she dials my father, using the points of her inch and a half rocket-red nails to punch in the numbers. If he's not in his office I'll probably be tossed out. Not because I look menacing, but because I look *strange*, and strange, at this law firm (and, I'm being reminded, Toronto) is not acceptable.

> "Yes, I'll send her right up. Traci? Your father is waiting for you. It's the fortieth floor dear, office 4057."

In case you were wondering, I get my sense of humour from my dad who, despite being a lawyer, is extremely funny. Or at least what I think is extremely funny. That thing with the swing and the cigarettes, very typical of my dad. Funny hee hee rather than funny ha ha. When I was nine, I had this humungous fight with my dad over whose *stuff* was whose. It started because I wanted to get him to leave my room. Privacy.

"This is *my* room," I said, "and you are sitting on *my* stuff so get out."

"You think this stuff is yours?" he replied, grabbing my sweater and hat. "This stuff is mine. I paid for it."

He was perfectly serious. My dad actually squeezed into my sweater and hat and walked downstairs.

"You know," he mused, plucking at the fluff on the sleeves, "it's odd but I feel just like a little girl."

"Aaagh, Dad, you're wrecking my Stuff! Mom!"

At this point my father, now in the kitchen making himself a peanut butter and banana sandwich, began to sing a little Beatles sweater song, just loud enough for me to hear. He has a habit of rearranging lyrics to popular songs of the seventies and eighties to fit current events.

"Igaddanew sweater yeah, yeah, yeah
Igaddanewsweater yeah, yeah, yeah
now I'm goin' down, to have myself some cereal
do do do do
I'm goin' down to have myself some cornflakes
do do do do
yeah I'm goin' down to have myseeeellllf
some cornflakes!
Yeah Yeah Yeah YEAH!"

Ha ha ha.

All total, my father has written twenty different songs to the tune of *She Loves You*. Ten are about me.

He wore my sweater around the house for days. It took me a week to forgive him for that particular incident, let alone get the very stretched-out sweater back. One thing about living with my dad, you have to have a pretty thick skin. And a sense of humour. His jokes can go on for a long time.

"Going up?" A demure man with glasses as thick as Coke bottles places his hand on the small of my back to guide me onto the elevator.

> Herded into a crowd of business men and women I'm choked by a sudden onslaught of Chanel No. 5.

> "Can you push floor forty for me please?"

A Knight in Shining Armour, A Bull in a China Shop

12:15 p.m.

It's too bad I harbour a distaste for the business district because I actually think men in suits are cool. I have a thing for the look and smell of newly pressed business suits, and inhale deeply on elevators filled with businessmen, bankers, lawyers and mobsters (just kidding). It's not a sex thing. It's more a control thing. Years of watching my father disappear out the front door in the morning in a crisp, newly dry-cleaned suit developed a deeply ingrained association between a sharp shoulder line and control, something my father always had. I liked control. When I was a kid, my father's suit meant he was a kind of superhero, fine wool and thick linen were his urban armour. I assumed my father went to work everyday to fight for the forces of good. Later, even after I realized he fought not for good but for money, I continued to believe his suit somehow made him invincible.

Ever since I was young enough to want to be anything I wanted to be just like my father: calm, cool, collected, and undeniably in control. No surprise, I suppose, to anyone who knows anything about family dynamics or psychology.

Once I told my Grade Two teacher, Mrs. Mable, that I wanted to be a lawyer like my dad because lawyers didn't cry. Lawyers had a sense of humour.

Back then, despite being a big cry baby myself, I was not a fan of criers. Or of rage, screaming, or instability. I was a fan of my father, the only person I had ever known who seemed relatively unaffected by my mother.

My dad wore his calm like his well-pressed suit: a glass bubble that surrounded him no matter what else was happening. He could walk into any situation and stand impervious, an angel in a soft, dark grey two-piece, and maroon tie. He could pick us up out of my mother's raging seas and drop us at the river's edge unscathed. My father was the only person who could look my mother in the eye when she was at her worst— and not blink.

I always blinked.

I was slightly afraid of my mother.

If my father was a rock, my mother was that rock candy, *pop candy*, we used to buy at the convenience store for the thrill of oral demolition. Slick plastic pockets with a smattering of sweet, sour dust that would blow your taste buds to pieces, as you sat on the porch and let them go to town on your tongue. Sizzle Pop *Kablam*. Rice Krispies on dextrose. Unlike my father, my mother favoured Cotton Ginny jogging suits and had no armour. Mom bruised easily, and deeply, shades of blue and purple you wouldn't think could naturally appear on a person. My mother's skin was a cellular mood ring, so sensitive the slightest breeze turned her lips a tender shade of eye-shadow blue. When my mother fell, huge welts popped up through her skin like the smooth mushroom heads on tree trunks in the forest.

It wasn't always like that. Before she met my father, my mother was a tough-as-nails dental assistant for a mean old dentist in Oshawa who swore, smoked Camels and called her "dear." She used to walk through dirty city mud puddles, trudging — with a steely resolve to keep her white shoes white — to a job where grown men bit her fingers. My mother also has moon-shaped scars on her thumb from a little girl who clamped down hard and wouldn't let go. Mom used to be a fighter, of tooth decay and more. When she met my father, at a friend's surf n' turf party in Toronto, she knew she would marry him and never wear thick white shoes again. She waited patiently for him to ask her, ready to pack up her things and kiss soggy cotton swabs goodbye. When, three years later, he finally did ask, she said "yes," and settled down to the career of family. Then my mother, once a fighter, gave birth first to me, then to my brother. Suddenly, and for the first time, she was afraid.

I once had a friend, Paula, whose father was a former Siamese twin, born joined to his brother at the hip, separated when he was two years old. Even after they separated, married, and were living in different hemispheres, whenever the brother fell, Paula's father would feel sharp phantom pains in his wrists, back, and legs, passed on long distance, like a collect call. One time his brother poured a cup of hot coffee in his lap and Paula's father couldn't stand up for a day.

I had my own phantom twin in my mother. She bruised when I fell, felt my pain in a way I couldn't control. Any damage inflicted upon either my brother or I was inflicted upon her, times three. My mother winced when I rode my bike, screamed ozone rippers when I tipped into the cement sidewalk, elbows first. My mother's hugs, when the Band-Aids were on snug, were monster clutches searching my little body for a sense of relief that wasn't there. Shortly after I turned eight, I lost interest in my bike and stopped letting my mother hug me.

I probably should have been grateful for a mother who would throw herself in front of a train for her children. Unfortunately, my only real memory of my mother in my early years is that she couldn't take a joke.

Which is a shame, because some of the funniest things that ever happened to me, happened because of my mother.

A good example is the time we drove the car into a bus. It was one of those hellish rainy days and I had coerced my mother into taking me to the mall to buy new sneakers. It was 5:30 p.m. and the mall was about to close. Being eight, I was angry because we wouldn't make it and the sneakers would be gone. Bradley, my brother, was four, easily agitated, and the perfect target because he was strapped in so tightly. He became the outlet for my raging mood. I began to hail a barrage of light punches on his leg. Just to bug him. Misery, especially when misery is eight, loves company. In the middle of my third round of punches, my mother snapped. If memory serves correctly, she *turned around while still driving* and — I swear — in her stress, made a motion I interpreted as an attempt to grab my head. We hit, though not at any outrageous speed, a parked bus. Though the immediate emotional impact was stressful (no one was hurt of course), afterwards the whole incident was pretty hilarious. The Bus Story is a personal favorite of mine. Not a favorite of my mother's. In fact, the one time my mother caught me telling the story, she burst into tears.

"It's *funny*," I said. I had yet to learn the first rule of comedy: tragedy plus *time* makes something really funny, especially if that something involves a car and a bus.

"She's right, Mary," my dad conceded. "It is funny."

"Oh sure, take her side. You're not the one people will think is crazy."

"Who says people will think you're crazy?" mused my father. "Hitting a bus isn't crazy, it's expensive."

Fending off awkward situations with humour is a particular personality trait. Whatever it's called, it should be named after my father, a master of using humour to avoid any kind of sincere discussion. For the longest time I thought avoidance was the way you were supposed to deal with emotional interactions.

"Just don't do it when your mother's around," my dad said. "Your mom's got a thin skin, she thinks you're making fun of her."

I was. He knew that. But more important to me was the difference my father set out between my mother and myself. Unlike my mother, I was supposed to have a thick skin.

And because I looked up to my father, because I wanted nothing else in the world than to be like my father, that *thick skin* was something I aimed for. Over the years, to my mind, it would prove useful.

A Dress for Every Occasion

12:18 p.m.

Today I learned it's not only intimidating to have a father who works on the fortieth floor, but also inconvenient. I ride the wrong elevator twice before I finally reach the right office. Once I get on an elevator that only goes to the thirtieth floor (and of course have to go all the way back down again). Then I get to the fortieth floor and am faced with all locked doors. (You have to take a specific elevator so you hit the desk that can let you in.) Tugging ruefully on the silver knob I can *feel* the metaphor coming on. If I were in a more superstitious mood I would take this as a sign and go back to the hotel. Instead, I zoom back down to ground zero. Sweating a job interview sweat, I am the least popular thing on the elevator. A secretary in a sailor suit actually avoids me, standing on the other side, as we rocket down. Smugly I wonder if she thinks I'm applying for a job.

"You work here?" I ask.

"Pardon?" Batting her thickly crusted eyelashes at me, sailor secretary allows herself to scan my person.

"You work here?"

"Yes." Her eyes float skyward. Sadly, the ceiling of the elevator is not mirrored. She has nothing to look at.

"Looks like a fun place to work."

"Well it's not." Jamming a French manicured nail into the button for the next floor, she jumps ship early.

Fuck you, I think with a smile. Maybe it's the tattoos. I bend my head and send negative cursing energy at her butt as the elevator door slams shut. I am semi-pagan, I only use my powers for defensive purposes.

At the office, my father is smug. "They thought you were Greenpeace," he says.

Ha ha.

"Do you remember that time I came in here in my tutu and they wouldn't let me up at all?"

"Actually that was me," my father admits, "I told them if you came in a tutu or a bear suit you weren't allowed in."

Ha ha.

"So, sushi or Chinese?" I ask.

"Where do you want to go?"

"Can we go to that place we went that other time?"

"Sure...." my father pauses, scans the mosaic of neat post-its on his desk. Finally, looking up with a smile, he pats his pocket, "Guess I'm buying, eh?"

Ha ha.

"I left my gold card at the hotel."

When I was ten my dad used to take me to a Chinese restaurant, one of the fancy ones, the Pink Pearl, every second Sunday of the month. It was *our time*, a scam my mother set up so that, once a month, she'd only have *one* hellish child to deal with. Our lunch followed one of those educational package deals that offered a year's worth of tickets for matinee concerts at Roy

Thompson Hall. Part of a program designed to introduce kids to classical music. If you ask me, introducing a child to anything by taking away their Sunday is a bad idea. I must have gone to twenty concerts and the only thing I can tell you about classical music is that the conductor's stick is called a baton and a clarinet and oboe are similar but not the same. Because the concerts were on Sunday, and downtown, my mother insisted I wear what would otherwise be my church clothes: a black skirt and stiff white blouse. Once a month I was wrapped in itchy wool, tied with ribbon and pushed onto the subway. The only good thing about the whole fiasco was that the concerts were close enough to merit my father taking me to Harbourfront, and the Pink Pearl for lunch. Then, as now, I lived for food, specifically the rows and rows of yummy sticky rice wrapped in steamed lotus leaf parcels that made the Pink Pearl famous. I spent the whole concert thinking about lunch, kicking the seat in front of me and mentally ordering my meal: placing the dainty white dim sum dishes in a perfect semicircle on the imagined white tablecloth.

I can only guess that my father's decision to go along with the plan was about more than my education around classical music. At ten, I was displaying what they call warning signs, little red flags which separated kids who sailed through grade school from turf like me. School was, in the simplest terms, *not going well*. By grade five I was the favoured target of merciless punishments by the popular kids who ran the all-girl private school I attended. I held special status somewhere between Loser and Pot Hole. The footprints in the small of my back were beginning to sting.

To this day, I'm not exactly sure why or how this happened. Like everyone else I was shy, but apparently I gave off some sort of pheromone that made my shyness an invitation for something more. I have a lingering suspicion my loser status might have been related to a lame, chipped-up Snoopy lunch box my mother made me bring to school the first day, thinking it was better than a paper bag. I hate to blame my social ineptitude on a lunch box, but there is the rule that once you're established as a geek, especially a lunch-box-toting geek, it's impossible to go back.

I will never forget the speech my mom gave me on my first day of school.

"Your problem," she said, "is that you don't smile enough. How about if you try to have a friendly and open attitude with everyone you meet today? Everyone you see today, you smile and say, 'How about we be friends?' How does that sound?"

I spent the entire day wandering around the schoolyard trying my new opening line. By the end of the day everyone thought I was crazy. What I should have done is lied and said I had a pony.

My schoolmates were more the pony and tennis club crowd.

They could have given a shit about my warm and friendly attitude.

Maybe there are no good reasons for being unpopular. But there are certainly consequences. Whatever the reason, I was soon stuck with the title outcast, unable to deal with the minefield of girls with blond ponytails and a sense of self-importance which I lacked. Year by year, I gave up on my warm smile and concentrated on not crying when I opened my locker to find streaks of lemonade from the juice boxes Jenny Smyth and her clan had taken to squeezing in through the vent. My math book had ants.

My feet grew heavy, the pavement on the driveway leading up to the school became sticky. It took an extra hour for me to walk to school.

In retrospect, I can't think what my mom could have possibly done to make things any better for me. She bought me a variety of Judy Blume novels, none of which helped. I didn't want to feel part of a teen crisis. I had no desire to know I was part of the cycle of life. I wanted solutions.

The answer I finally came up with was to simply *refuse* to go to school; I spent afternoons at the local corner store instead, reading magazines all day. When that didn't work, I tried to break my leg by *falling* off the garage roof. I half succeeded, spraining my ankle badly enough to cause my mother a minor heart attack. For my suicidal ineptitude I was granted two days off school, which I spent recuperating on the couch. Returning to school, I quickly learned that the only thing less socially acceptable than *trying* to mangle yourself, is trying and *failing*.

"Hey Traci! Next time you jump off a building, try landing on your *head*! It might improve your ugly face."

"Hey Traci, was that supposed to be some sort of Japanese kamakazi suicide dive?"

"Hey Traci! How come your locker smells like *lemonade*?"

Sitting across the table as I fingered the foam on my crutches, my father leveled with me.

"The thing is," he said, "people will always be mean and there's nothing you or your mother or I can do about it. You just have to live with it. Don't let them see you cry. Sometimes you have to have a thick skin, not let things get to you so much. Okay?"

"Okay."

"And Traci."

"Yes, Dad?"

"No more jumping off the roof. Okay?"

"Okay."

"That was dumb."

"I'm sorry."

"Well, you don't have to be sorry. You just have to be careful. You could have broken the roof."

I never jumped off the roof again. I turned to stone, smooth white stone like the cool walls of the convocation hall. I made my eyes mirror-blank so no one could see me. At recess, I retreated to the shady spot in the back of the schoolyard with a book and my lunch. I learned that being smart was a suitable explanation for being weird, and I became the best version of *smart* I could muster. The first lesson of being smart: always have a book in your hand.

I developed, as my father had suggested, an incredibly thick skin. In Grade Six, when Christy Spinet said Japanese people all had dandruff and smelled like rice, an argument that concluded with a slap to my face, I barely blinked. I gave a cold smile. Thoroughly freaked out, the popular kids took to merely despising me. They left me alone.

When I was twelve I started having intense papier mâché dreams. As I drifted off to sleep I would imagine cool strips of slimy paper being layered onto my skin, strip after strip, until I was thick with newspaper and paste. The mixture would dry up and pinch my skin. Encased in a hard shell, only two eyeholes allowed me to see out. Sometimes I would wake paralysed, my arms rigid at my sides, my leg muscles tense and achy. Sometimes I woke up still encased, something invisible but heavy on my chest, making breathing difficult. I viewed the world through tiny slits in my plaster body and wiggled my fingers to test my freedom.

Later, I had a dream I was confessing to my father, lying on my bed in my plaster body.

My father laughed and said, "In her dreams my daughter is a piñata."

Ha ha.

I would never deny the convenient significance of this dream.

My father might.

Spilt Milk

12:35 p.m.

The glitter I glued to my shoes during the ride from Montreal is flaking off on the sidewalk as my father and I march past across the river bed between the tall buildings to the water front. Sunlight catches the glittery trail I leave behind. Knowing how little my father likes walking and talking, I stay silent, turning every once in a while to watch my reflection in the mirrored walls of the building. I need a haircut maybe. My father is almost exactly a foot taller than me, which you can't tell, because I'm wearing platforms.

He's determined, arms swinging. It looks like I'm following him, rather than walking with him.

"Hey, spare some change?" The woman with the sign is almost hidden among a small mountain of sleeping bags and blankets.

I stop and dig in my purse. My father walks two or three more steps ahead before stopping.

"Friend of yours?" he asks, as we continue to walk forward.

"I liked her sign. It said, *goin' crazy, wanna come*?" My voice is loud. It always is. People turn to stare and an old woman shakes her head.

"Nice."

"I thought so."

I pause, let the silence sit between us for a while.

"Our family should get a little sign like that," I add.

My mother had the honour of being the first person in our family to have a nervous breakdown, one sunny morning as Bradley and I were preparing to go to school. May 16, 1987. I was eleven years old.

Things had been getting progressively worse in our family. On the outside, for public purposes, we were a relatively normal household. Not the coolest family on the block, but one of the nicest. Our grass was always cut and the walkway fenced with lilies my mother tended almost daily. The kind of family that had barbeques people came to because we did a good job of entertaining, and because we supplied the expensive beer our neighbours liked. We even had a sprinkler my brother and I would half-heartedly run through before retreating indoors for popsicles.

Inside, our family routine was less than entertaining.

By the time I was eleven, my house was one big boobytrap. Too many bruises had begun to fester beneath the surface of my mom's thin skin. The tenderness was like a mosquito bite that itches and itches and never fades away. Like in that *Tom And Jerry* cartoon, where Tom sets out a whole floor with mousetraps to catch Jerry, then, while he's backing out of the room, his tail flicks one of the traps and it's *pow pow pow*, hundreds of traps snap shut. Your typical household chain reaction. That was my house. I was Jerry. I was hyper-aware that the clumsiness of my fingers, the loudness of my voice all too often set off a reaction in my mother. I could be upstairs brushing my hair and *snap*, an explosion downstairs. It was that easy. My mother's anger sensed microwaves no one could see, especially not me. Not funny at all.

To this day, I associate nervous breakdowns with the smell of spoiled milk.

It was a bad morning. One of those mornings when mom didn't get dressed, when the very air around her felt so prickly and static we wouldn't go near her for fear of shock. Mornings like this, mom's face emerged from the bedroom puffed and swollen. Mornings like this I never looked my mother in the eye.

Sitting at the breakfast table I listened to her as she moved around the kitchen fixing breakfast. The edge of her housecoat dragged on the floor, collecting cat hair and what little dust was allowed to gather in the kitchen, as she pulled open drawers looking for something I could guess wouldn't be there. There was the aggravating sound of spoons and knives tripping over each other as they fell to the floor, already in trouble for being in her way. In the oven door I caught a glimpse of her reflection, a tuft of hair stuck up out of her otherwise tamed do like a shark's fin.

The fridge door swung open and a carton of milk toppled off the top shelf, landing on the floor with a plop and gurgle. Mom picked up the carton and gave it a sniff.

"Who put this milk in the fridge?"

My brother, who had been scrambling around the table looking for this and that in the sort of panicked frenzy that goes with being in grade school, stopped in his tracks. Slowly, like a doe in the forest who hears the sound of a branch breaking, I lifted my head. When my mom was mad it was always best not to move. Stay still and wait. I could hear my heart working itself into a tight fist in my chest. The hum of the fridge and the sound of sunlight pouring through the window filled the room.

"What, Mom?"

"Who put this here?"

A loaded question with no right answer. My brother and I remained frozen.

"What is wrong with you kids? Don't you listen? What is wrong with you kids? Goddammit! Am I alone here? Goddammit!"

It was hard to know if my mother was actually addressing us. Sometimes when she yelled like this she wasn't yelling at anyone. Sometimes she yelled at my Dad while she sat squeezing my hand. Sometimes I wasn't even sure if she knew I was in the room.

"But..."

She threw the milk carton out through the window. That and the vase, the dirty plates on the counter....

"Nothing I do is ever enough. Nothing I do is enough. You take and take and take. You think I want to sit here and do your dishes all day? You think that's what I am? Don't you think? Don't you care?"

She threw everything out: knives, forks, fruit, through the window, some of it missing and hitting the wall, *splat*. She pushed us out the door and locked it. Bradley sat down on the steps and cried, his pale little hand a fragile snowflake pressed against the door, as if, somehow, his will might open it. The morning air was cold and wet with spring. My ears rang with the angry and embarrassing sound of breaking glass. My face burned. Little words buzzed around me like fruit flies. No. No. No. This wasn't happening. Bradley's hand, weak and scared, was my undeniable proof that something had gone terribly wrong. We sat and waited outside for an hour, our bums cold ice cream scoops on the chilly stone steps. We waited for our mother to let us back in. When she didn't, I took that little hand in mine and went next door.

"My mother's locked us out." I told Mrs. Crown, our neighbour.

"Your mother did what?" Mrs. Crown had that awful habit of slightly mouthing your words when you talked to her. I found it extremely distressing and looked away.

"My mother locked us out. She's throwing stuff out the window. We need to call my father."

"What's your daddy's number?"

The number on the message board next to the phone. *For Emergencies Only*, that I had used once before, when mom locked herself in the car. His voice was tired.

"I'm coming to get you," he said.

Mrs. Crown fed my brother little pieces of apple he didn't want. I stood tiptoe on a phone book looking through the peephole, holding a glass of water she had given me. A cab pulled up and my father appeared, his blue suit and white shirt coming into focus as he walked up the steps, his top-half magnified so his head was as large as the rest of his body. I remember the smell of soap as my father took my hand and loaded me into a cab to take us to Aunt Ruth's house, away from my mother.

I don't know how he got my mom out of that house.

I don't think about it.

Later that week I heard Dad tell Bradley that sometimes people are like cars, they run out of the stuff that makes them run and they break down. Sometimes people need to get fixed.

Bradley asked me if this meant Mom was in a garage.

"She's not in a garage," I hissed, "she's in a hospital because she's a person."

"Dad said she was like a car."

Aunt Ruth said Mom had a *nervous breakdown*. She said that meant from now on we would have to be a little quieter. A little "better around the house."

Poor mom. Thin skin. We had to be brave. Keep our chins up. Dad had to work. I had to look after Bradley, tell him everything was okay.

"You have to have thick skin," I told him. "Don't cry. Okay?"

"Okay."

But Bradley cried every night, and so did I, though not when my father was within earshot. I cried into my pillow, tucked into the corner of my closet, my bare feet sticking out and my toes turning cold as my face grew hot with tears, tears so secret they stung and cut their way through my system. During school, when it hurt so bad I wanted to cry, I went to the bathroom, squatted with my feet on the lid and pinched the skin on my arms, staring at the graffiti on the wall until I was purple and tender. My mother's fears leaking into me, I thought, my mother's craziness sown into my guts, blossoming. I wanted to thump my chest and cough it out, but I couldn't. Even after my mother returned, five months later, softer and calmer, buffed smooth, a rage continued to grow inside me like an ugly pearl.

My thick skin will keep it in, I thought. I am not my mother.

"If you ever need anyone to talk to dear, you just let me know. It's okay to cry you know."

Three neighbours, two guidance counsellors, and a science teacher told me that. All I could think was, *everybody knows.*

Gotta have a thick skin.

40

Warning Signs

12:50 p.m.

The Pink Pearl, our Chinese restaurant of choice, is packed with the remnants of a family banquet, people spilling out as we squeeze in. The greasy, salty smell of Chinese food fills my lungs as I stand with my father, taking deep breaths of MSG. We wait in silence, avoiding eye contact with the people inside the restaurant. Every five minutes a cell phone rings and a customer stops eating to talk on the phone. Every five minutes I hear ring and edge a little closer to an early grave.

"I can't tell you how much I respect you for not getting a cell phone," I tell my Dad.

"Too expensive. I need to save my money to buy my daughter piercing and *tattoos*."

"Subtle Dad, real subtle. You're like a Zen master of the hint."

I can tell my dad is embarrassed being part of the odd couple at the restaurant. He in his shiny suit, me in my Raggedy Ann dress and fuzzy purple locks. He's only half joking about not letting me in the building wearing a tutu. He was pissed when I showed up for a visit in my ballet outfit last Christmas and refused to take me to any place with windows.

"What do you care?" I asked, hopping from ballet slipper to ballet slipper as we sped through the halls of his office. "It's my hair, my body, my skin."

"My money," he answered, though he never asked for any of it back. What's done is done. Mom says he just doesn't understand how I can look like I do. Mom understands a bit, I think, but she and I see eye to eye a little more often now.

"Table for two? Non-smoking?"

My dad raises an eyebrow. "Did you want to smoke?"

"Nah. Did you?"

"I quit. Too expensive, gotta pay for my kid's tattoos."

Did I mention my dad's jokes tend to be a tad on the repetitive side?

I can't help but feel a little exposed as we make our way to the table. Everything is so white here: tables, curtains, white light flooding in from the windows. I feel like I'm walking through an x-ray.

"If you're self-conscious," my dad notes when we sit down, "you should put a sweater on."

"How about we don't worry about what I look like and just order?"

"Fine."

My dad buries his head behind the tall menu, "Do you want to order a chow mein or do you just want to have dim sum?"

"Let's just have a nice pleasant father-daughter lunch."

"So dim sum, then?"

My shrink says nervous break-downs don't just happen, they build up, fester, then explode. People break down not because they're weak, but because something inside is *weakening* them. I've always imagined a large tumor building below the surface of the skin until it's so big you can't function any more, and it finally bursts.

In grade nine I had a lump in my neck for three weeks during winter exams. I kept feeling it on my neck and thinking "That's odd, feels like a golf ball."

In my dreams it was a pearl, shining through my skin. A pearl as big as the rock on Wilma Flintstone's necklace. Two days after exams, while shopping with my father, I collapsed with fever. A very serious case of strep throat. I spent a day in the hospital.

"You felt an egg on your neck and you didn't think to worry?" The doctor raised an eyebrow. So did my mother.

"Do you want to talk?"

In the years after her return from the hospital, my mom became a professional talker with the help of her shrink, Kathy. Mom worked *through* her bruises now. Therapy gave her the power some draw from God, along with a similar zealotry and aura. My mom transformed into the neighborhood confessor. Housewives flocked to her for home-baked therapy. Through my teens, our house became a haven for the needy and depressed housewives of North Toronto.

My mother was a steaming bowl of sympathy who understood that a nice car and a set of matching kids doesn't necessarily make you a happy person.

"My husband won't talk to me."

"I'm just not *motivated*."

"Is it wrong to be sad?"

"There, there. Talk about it."

"I hear you."

Gag.

I could see them coming a mile away, in their flowered shirts, matching skirts, and white shoes, always ringing the doorbell and asking to speak to my mother under the guise of *borrowing a cup of sugar* or a recipe for gingerbread. Twenty minutes with my mother and they were crying like soap stars, confessing dark thoughts while Mom poured.

"One lump or two dear? Now, now. Let it all out."

I wanted nothing to do with my mother's circus of confession and release and avoided the crying women curled around glasses of Merlot looking like baby birds fallen from nests. I wouldn't even bring in the box of Kleenex. I left it by the door.

My sentiment was shared by the rest of the family. The cat hid upstairs with my dad in his study, the dog curled up under my brother's bed. I slothed, mute and boneless, in front of the TV in the basement, listening for the sound of her timid footsteps on the stairs. The approach.

"Honey? Honey did you want to talk? About anything? Honey you know you have to talk more. Work *through* your problems. Don't keep that bad stuff bottled up inside."

I didn't think my mother wanted to hear what I had to talk about.

Since my fifteenth birthday all I could think about was the fact that I couldn't sleep anymore because I was afraid of silence. Silence was my enemy. At night, I would sneak down in my pajamas and sleep in front of the television, just to hear the sound of something other than the empty ringing in my head. The hollows of my head had become like nightmares I had as a child, where silence always preceded a strange marching noise. Something wicked this way comes. Something unseen and unseeable lurking in the darkest corners of my mind, ready to advance on silence. Sometimes I would sit alone and shake, convinced the tremors were earthquakes predicting an eruption.

During my mother's reign as self-help guru, I progressed from pinching and poking myself with a knitting needle to cutting. By sixteen it was my habit to sit in the closet and cut into my legs with oily smelling Bic blades that burned when they sliced. At night the backs of my thighs would stick to the sheets as my head screamed with pain. At first I cut when I was at my worst. Later I cut every night, everywhere. I cut deep enough to see the bone in my fingers, long enough to circle my ankle. I cut so that it hurt to walk to school, my socks and shoes rubbing the sore red lines on my feet as I darted through the back entrance to the school to avoid prayers.

I cut to assure myself I was in control. I cut into my thick skin to relieve the pressure bubbling underneath. I had thick skin. And it was slowly ripping apart.

Want to talk about that, Mom?

At school they called me 'The Mummy' because I was always covered in bandages. I scratched the insides of my ears with paperclips so they would be red to avoid swim class and wore long sleeves, even in summer. I was a master of disguise. I could also, miraculously, pretend to be happy. My only friend, Katie Tether, a fellow nerd whose claim to fame was a pair of eyeglasses thicker than the average finger, was the only one I told about my habit.

"Don't ever ask me about it," I said, when she finally caught sight of a particularly brutal scratch that stretched from my wrist to my elbow, "it's nothing."

Katie, not used to any kind of confession between us, didn't talk to me for a week after that. When she finally called again to see a movie, we silently agreed not to discuss it.

Ironically, the only person to ever confront me about it was my religious education instructor.

"God knows all your secrets," she told me, "all will eventually be revealed."

I can't help wondering if my life might have changed dramatically if the physics or math teacher, rather than the religion teacher, had heeded me with a warning.

In the Family Way

1:00 p.m.

The Pearl is quiet and serene with only the white noise of couples talking in neutral tones. There's no fighting over dim sum. My father is infinitely comfortable here, the only conflict in sight is the rough texture of the lake beyond our window table.

I remember once, when I was seven or so, my father took us to a family Italian restaurant downtown. It was one of those really corny places where you pay $7.95 for a small plate of spaghetti and a huge helping of atmosphere. The wall was covered in bells and whistles the waiters could start with a push of a button when it was someone's birthday. It wasn't my birthday so nobody pushed the bells and whistles for me, which was probably good because it was apparently everyone else's birthday that night and the bells were going nonstop. At the table next to me a little boy was having a birthday party and all his friends had gathered around him to pat him on the back and give him plastic presents.

Lots of trucks.

Then, just as my bother and I were soaking up the last of our spaghetti drool with our oily garlic bread, I heard a scream. The little boy was standing on the table, clutching a plastic robot and crying. My mother said someone had just tried to move it to clear the table.

My father bristled. "If either of you kids ever screamed like that I'd have you in the car faster than you could fart."

I wondered if that meant farting in the restaurant would be O.K.

I also wondered, briefly watching the little boy's mother and father bicker over how to deal with the screaming child, if that little boy's parents ever cried and screamed at home. I already had a strange concept of domains. Tiny invisible countries where it was O.K. or not O.K. to cry and scream. Maybe it was better to do it at a restaurant, surrounded by bells and whistles.

My dad is annoyed by noise. I'm afraid of silence. The scariest things happen when you're all alone and the only noise is your own shallow breathing.

It seems highly unfair to me that my brother would not re-member the day my mother had a nervous breakdown or any of the insanity that preceded it. But my brother's memories are fused with the updated version of my mom. He isn't plagued by the odour of sour milk, something that lingers whenever my mother reaches her hand out to me. My brother is more inclined to connect my mother with the aroma of cookies and coffee and other symbols of motherly goodness.

My brother does not remember mother's nervous breakdown.

"Traci?"

He remembers mine.

"Go away."

My brother, home early from basket-ball practice, stood slouched on the threshold of limp and stone, his jaw slack. He stared at me.

"What are you doing?"

Sitting on the black and white check linoleum bathroom floor, my back pressing the cupboard and my foot pushed against the toilet for support, I was managing, somehow, to lose my balance. Later I would learn I was suffering from shock. Some-thing to do with the stream of blood pouring out of my arm.

"Oh my God," I whispered, "Oh my God." My mind raced with ways to cover up. I had a brief flash of sewing my own arm, accompanied by another flash of such intense pain I thought I would never breathe again. A set of cold hands was taking turns poking cold fingers into the pink of my insides.

"Hurts," my body moaned, "hurts."

"What are you doing?" Bradley shrieked, his voice thin and brittle kindling.

Sounds began to melt. Bradley's equipment bag crashed to the floor. He raced out of sight. I flexed my hand and the blood flowed faster.

"Shit."

Bradley's face reappeared, large and sweaty. He was screaming, pushing towels onto my arm.

The weight of my brain shifted to the base. I slowly slipped sideways. My skull connected with the cold hard tile of the bathroom floor.

Black.

It amazes me that when people find out about this sort of thing, the first question everyone asks is *"Why?"* We're a society of need-to-knows. Everyone wants to see the movie of the week and hear the expert testimony, all in attempt to explain the act that goes against the basic human instinct, to survive. Imagine if I had died. Everyone would have been furious, not that I was dead, but that I didn't leave a note.

What are we supposed to tell your parents?

What are we supposed to read at your funeral?

What are we supposed to put in the school newspaper?

The truth?

It was like watching a big hairy spider crawl up someone else's wall.

I slipped. Cut a gash in my arm an inch deep.

But it was an accident.

It was a mistake, I told them. It was a mistake.

It's not like I want to die.

DEAR FRIENDS & FAMILY,

PLEASE EXCUSE MY ACTIONS ON THE AFTERNOON IN
QUESTION. I CAME HOME FROM SCHOOL AND
EVERYTHING WAS WRONG. I LOOKED AROUND MY
HOUSE, THE EMPTY TEA CUPS IN THE KITCHEN,
THE TABLE WHERE I SAT WHEN MY MOTHER DECIDED
SHE'D HAD ENOUGH, AND I FELT ANGRY AND SAD. TOO
ANGRY AND SAD. SO I WENT UPSTAIRS AND I FOUND
MY RAZOR BLADES.
MAYBE I WAS ~~THING~~ THINKING ABOUT GOD, OR MY
HAIR, OR DYLAN AND BRENDA.
MAYBE I WAS THINKING

no one understands me.

IN ANY CASE I APOLOGIZE FOR ANY INCONVENIENCE.
PLEASE GO ABOUT YOUR BUSINESS AND, IF YOU
FEEL SAD, TALK TO MY MOTHER. ☺

YOURS,

Traci

No one believed me.

"I'm not crazy," I said. Stupid assholes. "I'm not staying here either."

Stuck in a mud puddle of cold faces, I flailed hopelessly against the strength of nurses who pinned me with iron-strong white hands. A mobile of upside-down faces blocked my view. Talking chins lectured me to lie still, help myself.

"Where's my dad?" I whispered.

"Just lie back."

"I said where's my dad?"

Good things come in pairs.

For the second time in his life, my father was committing a member of his family.

Ward Seven's Singing Sensation

1:09 p.m.

It is decided that the safest subject for lunch conversation is the life of Bradley, who recently won his high school's economics competition and is off to the provincials. You can tell Dad's excited because he's not making fun of it.

"It's a pretty big deal," he says, as if this were news he is just now reading off a brochure, "it's the whole province."

"Hence the title, provincial."

"Yep."

"Sounds exciting."

Bradley is the only high school boy I know with his own business. I was the first person in my school to get a tattoo. You can see the range I'm dealing with. Sure it bugs me, I admit it. Though maybe only now, sitting with my dad, munching on oily shrimp roll cigars with nothing to talk about but Bradley wanting a new hard drive for his graduation. I asked for a red leather jacket.

You see, even then my dad and I had split off.

When my dad looks across the table and says he questions my career choice I know it's more than that.

I never considered the possibility of becoming a rock star until I landed in Ward Seven, the psych ward of one of Toronto's Sick Kids Hospital. Truthfully, at that age, I hadn't considered the possibility of becoming anything. Aspirations had always seemed whimsical and vulnerable. I had no desire to roam in a land that offered a bounty of potential disappointment. In my adolescent wisdom I figured I was more likely to follow in my father's footsteps: take a job I hated, with a huge salary as reward. But after only one day in the hospital, I knew that was no longer possible.

"I'm just a rock,
In an asy-y-y-lum,
In ward 7 there's no pain,
And the inmates never cry."

I sang my twisted Simon and Garfunkel lyrics on an endless cycle.

"You know," my father said, back turned away as he unpacked my few belongings and set them out on the dresser of my new room, "If you're trying to prove you're crazy, this is probably the fastest way to go about it."

"What would you rather I sing?"

Silence sat like an uneasy third wheel between my father and I. Finally he said, "The Beach Boys," because my father always says "The Beach Boys" whenever anyone asks him what kind of music he wants to hear.

"Brian Wilson went insane."

"Sing Beatles stuff then."

"Fine." I tried to launch into a rough version of "Helter Skelter" and quickly realized I didn't know the words.

So I screamed.

My father left the room, shoulders stiff as a scarecrow.

The silence in the ward was reminiscent of the silence of the high school exams I was missing. When I stopped singing I could feel the silence closing in on me. I scattered sounds in defense. If I wasn't singing I was tapping, sometimes randomly, listening and assessing different echoes that went with the different surfaces and textures; sometimes rhythmically, drumming out the beats of old seventies disco tunes, my heartbeat.

Slapping my skin, watching my scars shiver with the vibration, I began to sing, my voice pushing out of me, bouncing off the ceiling, floating out the window.

I could sing.

I'd always had the notion, until then, that I might be a good singer. At one point, I tried out for the choir and was accepted, but reneged when I found out how much practice was required. That, and I had to wear short sleeves to performances.

I surprised myself by being a rather good singer. Not in the Whitney Huston category, at least passable in what I would now call the Courtney Love section.

Still.

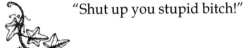 "Shut up you stupid bitch!"

"Shut up before I come over there and stuff my fist down your throat!"

Several of my ward-mates asked to be moved.

Sometimes I would think of my dad and sing his favorite Beach Boys songs.

When my dad sang Beach Boys songs, goofy and over-dramatic, dancing around my mother as she wept over the dirty dishes, it was a jibe and a joke. I sang them to myself. Long and soft, serious and mournful. For the first time, despite having failed biology, I could picture my insides, my lungs pumping out air, turning into sound, into words. I imagined that as I breathed in and exhaled my lungs were hugging my heart. A suitable explanation for the way singing made me feel.

"It makes you feel better?" doctors asked.

"Whole," I answered, "three dimensional. Like I've always been this way, I just never noticed before."

"You never felt three dimensional before?"

Dementia.

"No," duh, "I just never thought of it before."

Denial.

I steadfastly refused to see my mother. My father, when he visited, maintained a calm demeanor you might associate with a North American businessman visiting the Third World. He made quiet jokes at the expense of my surroundings, sat uncomfortably in a plastic chair in the visiting room.

"You know," he mused one afternoon, "if I was going to paint a mental institution, I don't think I would paint it *white*. At least not all white. Don't you think white walls are kind of nutty?"

"You know, I don't think the word 'nutty' is commonly used around here. Besides I think the white is supposed to make you feel calm."

"Do you feel calm?" My father's eyes bounced around the room like a hungry kitten, circling the corners and around the doorway.

Hiding my arms, exposed by the skimpy hospital robe, I frowned. "Do I look calm?" I wanted him to look at me, frightened more by the fact that in a room devoid of everything but a cloudy glass window, my father could still manage not to look at me.

"You look a little drawn. Are you eating well?"

"I eat what they give me."

"What else do you do?"

"Sing."

He looked disappointed. Was he expecting me to be building up a business portfolio or arranging for study hall when I got out?

"I am a ROCK, in the as-y-y--y-lum!"

Most people I could blast out of the room with my singing. Doctors were the exception to this rule. For them my singing was a sign. Something worth writing about. The more I sang the more they wrote. Mostly I piped down in their presence.

If I was really stuck I would sit and try to dig out old lyrics stuck in the back of my brain. Mostly all I could remember were scraps of old hymns from school prayers.

"Dance then…"

"Traci?"

"…wherever you may be… I am the Lord of the Dance…said… he… I'll lead you all…

"Your mother was hospitalized when you were younger, for a nervous breakdown, wasn't she?" A stern looking psychiatrist peered over the twin arcs of his iron frames and eyed me suspiciously. The cool tile stuck to my feet as I padded around in front of the window. You're supposed to wear slippers in the ward but mine always seemed to fall off.

"Dance then!
Wherever you may be!
I am the Lord of the Dance
Said he!"

I could picture the rows of girls in uniform shifting weight from leg to leg, concealing gum in cupped palms. Lisa Channing said it was sacriledge for me to sing hymns because everyone knew all Asians were Moonies.

"Traci? Would you say that was a traumatizing period in your life?"

"I survived."

"Does that have any connection with the fact that you refuse to see your mother now?"

"No. I don't think so."

"Who do you think you're protecting?"

"Do I have to be protecting anyone?"

No answer.

I let the silence sit until it was clear this was not a rhetorical question, even though it was.

"Maybe I'm protecting myself. I don't know."

"From your mother?"

I had a sudden flash of my mother curled up on the kitchen floor, sun on her face, surrounded by bruised fruit and broken dishes. Sun streamed through the window of the hospital room and I held out my hand to collect the light in my palm.

"What are you thinking about?" the doctor asked.

"Breakfast," I sighed.

> *"I'll lead you all*
> *Wherever you may be*
> *I will lead you all in the dance said he."*

 One night, I had a dream I was walking in my grandmother's rose garden in Connecticut. In my dream, it was warm and the sun made the roses glow like holy streetlights. The earth was warm and soft and the stalks of the rose bushes didn't stick me as I clutched to them for balance. Suddenly a cold spray hit my back and I fell on my knees. I screamed at my mom to stop spraying me and tried to turn around, hands out front, and walk towards her, but the water pumped furiously. *Stop*! As I turned and faced the spray my dad's face peered out between the sun and water. The jet stream from the icy hose pounded my chest.

I woke up screaming and laughing hysterically, rocking in my bed as a nurse held my hand.

"It's nothing," I said, "it's just a joke."

Magnets

1:21 p.m.

It turns out my father does have a cell phone. I feel robbed. Here I was thinking he was at least above carrying a phone with him everywhere he goes and he's not. He's taking a call while I silently slip my little chopstick holder into my knapsack.

It's not stealing if I leave an extra tip when the check comes.

If my father leaves an extra tip.

Whatever.

I'm inclined to take out my little notebook and pretend it's a cell phone. Mentally I dial the Psychic Alliance and seek advice.

"Lunch is going O.K. I feel six years old sitting here with my father. I'm the only one in the whole restaurant who's not wearing black or grey. The food is really good though. I just stole a chopstick holder that looks like a dragon licking it's tail. Do you think I'll grow up and be famous or work at the bagel store for the rest of my life?"

"What?" my father asks, slipping his phone back into his briefcase, "What did you say?"

Slipping my pretend phone back into my pretend briefcase, I smile. "I said eat your dumpling."

I got out of the hospital the day of my brother's big game. My parents came to pick me up with a fresh change of clothes in hand and an angry sibling in the car. I saw his bent head from across the parking lot, staring down at the basketball in his lap. Driving home, Bradley, now Brad, focused his attention on the pimply surface of the ball, never once looking up, his body squished as far from me possible. I sat, body frozen in the seat as my stomach did angry flip-flops.

A strange cotton-ball-quiet separated us into compartments and no one spoke for a long time.

 I resisted the urge to sing.

Finally Brad raised his head.

"I just want to know if you're still going to go," he hissed between the two front seats.

"Maybe when we see how Traci's feeling," my mother whispered.

"Well how is Traci feeling then?" Brad said, slamming his body back against his seat.

"Umm," I coughed, "you could *ask* me."

Bradley ignored me and turned his body to face the window. All I could see was an angry back. Unaware of my plight, the weather was irritatingly sunny and cheerful. Laser beams of sunlight bounced off the cars and ricocheted into my eyes.

"Do you want to go see Bradley play?" my mother asked.

No suggestion could be less appealing. Slumped in my seat, I faked a yawn.

"I think I just want to sleep for a while. Why don't you go?"

"Sure?" My father peered at me through the rear view mirror.

"I'm fine. Really." I let my body radiate the message loud and clear. *Go. Please. Leave me alone.*

Later, pulling out of the driveway, my father paused and looked at me.

"Should we be taking the kitchen knives?" he asked.

I was alone.

There has never been a house as quiet and unsettling as mine was the day I arrived home from the hospital. Moving through the rooms of what had been my home, since I was four, I felt foreign and uninvited. The carpet was too sticky and soft under my feet. Walls overly grey and rough, ceilings too high. Didn't there used to be a tree outside this window? Squatting on the counter, the cat turned his head quizzically as I paced the floors as if to ask, "Do I know you?"

"Probably not," I answered, and with an indifferent flick of her tail, the cat turned her ass to me and fell asleep.

Nice. I headed upstairs.

Before I left, my room was a disgrace of disorder, littered with papers and laundry. Opening the door, I realized my space had been sanitized and re-ordered, papers swept into invisible corners, a new pink bedspread laid out, new pink curtains hung. A tiny pink rug covered the floor which my socks and underwear used to occupy. A little pink sweater lay on the pillow. For a second I wondered if my parents had found a neater, pinker person to replace me. As I turned to close the door, I spotted a tiny bouquet of pink rosebuds on my desk.

Traci,
Get Well Soon.
Love,
Mom

I closed the door and headed to the bathroom.

In the bathroom I felt strangely calm. Toeing the tiles, I wanted to look for a blood stain in the grout but resisted. Instead, I hooked my finger into the neck of my top and slowly pulled off my shirt. There's something very liberating about the privilege of undressing after weeks of wearing a gown you have to tie with strings at the back. I stripped off my clothes and soon stood in a puddle of my Sunday best. For months I had avoided mirrors, taking only the occasional glance at my face in the front hallway mirror to check my hair. At the hospital they made me look at my arms and tell them how I felt, but no one had made me look in the mirror. My stomach churned as I lifted my chin and opened my eyes. I looked like a zebra. Scars ranging from a pale pink to a sharp crusty red striped my skin. I looked grotesquely wrinkly.

"Oh my God, that's actually disgusting. Holy shit."

I ran myself a hot bath and stepped in. It felt like dipping my muscles in boiling water.

"Ouch, ouch, fuckin' ouch!"

I forced myself in, forced myself to sit down.

"Fuck! Fuck! Fuck!"

Finally, when it felt like I would rip apart at the seams I leapt out, wrapped myself in a towel, and padded into my pink pink room, steam oozing off my skin. Grabbing a pen and paper from my father's study I wrote in my journal, in the smallest letters I could,

This is what it feels like to feel everything.

Hearing the front door open, I slipped under my pink sheets and pretended to sleep.

"I could be anywhere," I whispered into my pillow, "but I'm home. Do you know me?"

As a general rule, precious little is expected of newly released psychiatric patients. Out of the hospital, I was told not to worry about exams and just enjoy my vacation. The religious education teacher sent a note in a little card with a lily on it inviting me to call her at home if I wanted to talk. I took that under advisement.

Pressure for a summer job quelled as I enjoyed a course of rest and relaxation, concentrating on doing nothing. Stress, my parents were told, was probably a contributor to my mental breakdown. Better for everyone if I was allowed to recoup before returning to school. I took this to mean I had the equivalent of the flu and treated myself accordingly, taking to bed.

My father, who refused to confront me to my face, could be heard through my vent, *venting* his frustrations about my recovery at my mother.

"When he said that she should *relax*," he reasoned, "I don't think he was referring to every muscle in her body."

"She needs replenishing space," my mother insisted. "She's very delicate right now."

To my mother, *delicate* meant special status. The mere mention of the word made my father's thick skin crawl. Hearing her use it in reference to *me*, the way she had so often used it in reference to her housewives, caused me to be overcome with mortification. I buried my sleep-swollen head between pillows and commanded my brain to dream. But the only thing I saw when I closed my eyes was black. Nothing. For the first time, my brain had no dreams to give me, unable to imagine beyond the reach of its own grey matter. I sputtered through sleep and woke sleepier the next day.

I'm fish-bowled, I thought, making my second visit to my front window one morning. My father once told me that goldfish have so little memory they don't feel sad trapped in their little bowls. But what if those little fish are sad to begin with? Imagine a million five-minute lifetimes of sad in a glass bowl. I'm fish-bowled. I can't imagine anything but this.

Another repercussion of mental illness, though short-lived, was that suddenly, for the first time in a long time, I had friends. This was partly because for a certain time no one knew what had happened to me; stragglers of curious classmates came to visit, looking for scars and IV's. It was the rumour, for a while, that I had cancer.

"Your friends are here," my mother would call.

"I don't have any friends," I hissed from my room, refusing to leave my bed.

"Sure you do. Chrissy. Chrissy's your friend. She's downstairs waiting for you."

"Tell her I don't have leukemia," I hollered, "tell her I'm crazy. See if she still wants to be my friend."

Some stayed. For those that did I was required to haul my tender body out onto the porch for lemonade provided by my mother, and shade provided by the backyard maple. They fidgeted uncomfortably while I smoked and twisted the bottoms of my t-shirts.

"So, do you feel better now?"

"Oh yeah. I mean, sure. I guess."

Staring into one awkward gaze after another, it occurred to me that I had no friends. More than once I paused to wonder why an awkward recluse who refused to leave the confines of her house and had tried to K-I-L-L H-E-R-S-E-L-F was so fucking interesting. I had the sneaking suspicion I was good-deed-of-the-month for my high school class.

"I never thought you were sad."

"I was."

I shooed them out after half an hour of small talk. All they did was remind me who I had been: smart and cold. And who I was now: diseased and shrunken. Sitting with them drained too much energy. Every visit required pulling on a skin that was already too small. After just a few weeks, my old self pinched the new me, still soft in the tender stage of molting. It was all I could do not to grab them by the shoulders and shake them and scream, "Do you know who I am? Because I'm not sure. The person who I was could never be like this, but here I am. You see my dilemma?" Instead, I said, "Is it hot out here?" or "More lemonade?" Then booted them out with feeble excuses and feigned headaches. After each visit, I crawled back into my cool cubicle house and curled up on the couch. Safe for the moment.

If my house was my sanctuary, my sanctuary was riddled with tension. The walls and floors oozed with the rawness of a fresh asphalt scrap. My family had become magnets, attracting and repelling, pushing each other through the corridors. My mother pushed towards me, a victim to take care of on a permanent, in-house basis. My father removed himself, vanishing behind closed doors when I approached. My brother followed suit and avoided the common rooms I frequented. Dinner, the one time the whole family inhabited the same space, was a badly rehearsed comedy routine performed for an angry audience.

"Pass the beans."

"So Traci, what did you do today?" my father would ask.

"Nothing."

My brother coughed.

"Shut up."

"Did you even go outside?"

"*Ha!*" My brother. The Heckler.

"No."

"Maybe you could do some prep work for school?"

Silence.

"Traci?" My mother's voice a mosquito in my ear.

"Just let me eat, okay?" I snapped, louder than I intended. Lately, when things turned to shouting, which they did increasingly, it was at my behest.

Bradley slammed his fork down on the table. "Why do you have to turn everything into a big deal? Like you have cancer or something and you have to make everything into a big drama. It's such bullshit."

"Fuck you."

My father stood and left the table.

"Please don't swear at the dinner table." My mother sighed.

"Excuse me? I'm getting chastised by someone who isn't even old enough to have his driver's license. I think that merits a little swearing."

"You make me sick." Bradley spat, his eyes two deep cuts in his face.

"Oh yeah, what part of me? My elbows make you nauseous?"

"Traci!" My mother's eyes darted between us. My body tensed

with the desire to lunge. My mother sensed this, and laid a hand on my shoulder.

"Don't *touch* me," I screamed.

"Why do you have to be such a basket case?" Bradley spat. "Why do you have to be such a freak? You know, everyone else in the family has pulled it together. Everyone except *you!* You're embarrassing."

"Fuck you. You don't even fucking know what you're talking about."

"Why can't you just be *normal*?"

"Asshole."

"I hate you."

And before I could say anything else he tore off, my mother close on his tail. Folding my hands on my lap, I put my head down on the table and sobbed.

Of course I knew why he hated me.

And how he hated me.

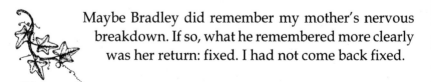 Maybe Bradley did remember my mother's nervous breakdown. If so, what he remembered more clearly was her return: fixed. I had not come back fixed.

If anything, I decided, I was even more broken than before.

Worse.

Marked beyond scars.

The steak on my plate, still emitting a musty odor, was raw and slimy. Looking down at the scars I cradled in my lap, and back up at the steak, I grimaced. The pink was a startling match. Yuck.

Back to bed.

Pulling myself step-by-step up the staircase, I was nearly blown off as my brother swept down to the ground floor, still trailed by Mom.

"Just send me away," he screamed, "send me to summer camp, send me to Grandma's."

"I'm going to bed," I whispered.

"At 7:00?" Mom asked.

"You see what I mean? It's like she has cancer! You don't go to bed before 8:00 unless you're still in *diapers*."

"Watch me," I hissed, slamming my door.

"Send me away or I'll leave!" Bradley shouted. So they did.

Two days later Bradley slipped onto a bus to Young Entrepreneurs in Ottawa. I hid in the basement. With Bradley gone I could sing whenever I wanted.

As my parents paced the floors upstairs, I let my vocal chords loose. Not knowing, not really caring, whether anyone was listening.

Kill Your Parents?
Start a Band.

1:40 p.m

It's no fun being the only person in an expensive downtown Chinese restaurant with zebra print stockings and three inch platform boots. Throughout lunch a predictable pattern has been developing, business men and women passing the table and scanning my outfit as they walk by.

"You ever wonder why it is no one in Toronto ever looks you in the eye? Like, they'll look *at* you but not...at you?"

"Maybe people would be more interested in looking you in the eye if you didn't have blue hair and jungle tights."

"It's indigo, not blue. Are you saying people won't look me in the eye because I have cool tights? Is that a comment about them or about my tights?"

No answer.

I'm not all that worried about my clothes drowning my personality. As I mentioned, I have a very loud voice, it carries further than the loudest stockings. It carried me all the way to Montreal and back.

It started that summer after I got out of the hospital. One day, I was wasting away in the basement, when my father shouted down the stairs, "Traci! Someone's here to see you."

Upstairs, a long, lanky, nervous boy stood in the doorway. His hair, the same shade of black as mine, contrasted harshly with his fair complexion. The last time I'd seen Jeff he'd been a string bean little kid trying to get a tan on his parent's porch using an empty record jacket covered in tin foil. Apparently Jeff had developed into a string bean Goth boy who had abandoned any desire for a tan.

"Hi."

"Hi."

"I heard you singing. You must really like the Beatles, huh?" Jeff smiled a shy little smile.

"Yeah, I do." Wow, I thought, I must be loud.

"You're pretty good. I mean, for someone in suburbia."

"Thanks."

"Listen, I know this sounds lame and every-thing, but I've got this, like, band, right? And we need someone for vocals. I don't suppose you'd be interested. It's mostly covers, we don't really write our own stuff yet."

"Uh-huh."

"Cool."

I could hear my mother rustling up the lemonade and cookies in the kitchen. Better get Jeff out the door as soon as possible.

"When?"

"Thursdays." Jeff raised an eyebrow as he took in my ensemble. Khaki shorts and a t-shirt. Not exactly your typical rock star outfit. But what you might expect from someone who spent all day in the basement singing the Beatles and playing Nintendo. "You've never sung with a band have you?"

"No."

"No biggie. Just come by on Thursday around seven. We sometimes order food after."

"Great." As I closed the door I did a teeny weeny Snoopy dance around the carpet. Oh my God, I thought, something cool is happening to me. Get right the fuck out of here.

"That's exactly what she needs," I heard my mom saying to my father that evening as I ravaged my closet for something to wear that wasn't entirely embarrassing. "A boyfriend."

Not in these clothes.

The next day I took my first excursion out of the house, a beeline downtown to Kensington Market, home of the teenage makeover. At home, the entirety of my old wardrobe, with the exception of my school uniform and a couple t-shirts, was sitting in a garbage bag on the curb. Seeing the sagging bag on the corner, my mother smiled at me from the window. Later my father told me she thought I'd cleaned up my room and taken the garbage out.

Ha ha.

It seems odd to me now that, inhaling the sandalwood and mothball cloud that surrounded Kensington Market, I had such a clear vision of what I wanted.

Moreover, I knew almost exactly where I would find it. Bypassing innumerable racks of worn black jeans and Metallica t-shirts, I headed straight for what my father later described as my Miss Hawaii get-ups: dresses with huge blossoms and bright colours that were to become my smocks of choice, mostly reds and purples, sometimes pinks and blues. I grabbed a handful of Hawaiian shirts for five dollars and matched them with two fluffy square dancing skirts I snatched for a twenty. Perfect. To make sure my underwear wouldn't show when I twirled, I picked up a dozen pairs of old fashioned bloomers from a shop without a sign. To this day I find it hard to criticize anyone's wardrobe because everyday I wore the tutu and Hawaiian shirt combo I looked at myself in the mirror and thought "I look great."

"Thank you for being a friend
Travelled down the road and back again
Your heart is true
You're a pal and a confidant."

It must say something about the strength of my voice that I sang a TV theme song for my audition and was still accepted into the band. Clutching a taped up mike with a shaking hand it was the only song I could remember off the top of my head. I had planned to sing something by Cindi Lauper, but there in Jeff's basement the only lyric that wasn't twisted up at the bottom of my stomach was the theme song from *The Golden Girls*. Cool. Thank God I had the many folds of my skirt upon which to wipe my sweaty palms. Opposite me, on a ratty yellow couch that was missing a huge bite out of the arm, a jury of dour Goths sat with arms crossed and *I'm soooo unimpressed* stapled to their faces by various piercings. I finished my song and cradled the microphone to my chest, waiting. Jeff smiled.

"Do you sing, like, real music?" asked Jude, a hollow looking boy with two heavy stripes of eyeliner under each eye.

"Oh! I mean, yeah, I just don't know them by heart, right? But I could sing almost anything I think."

"Your voice is really strong. Are you always going to wear those outfits?" A pointy-faced guy I recognized from before private school scrutinized my pink shirt with skepticism.

"No," Jeff cut in, "It's cool, you know, it's like she doesn't fit it. Like she's this freak who's, like, separate from us."

I decided Jeff was a man ahead of his time. A visionary. The others, quick to follow Jeff's lead (it was, after all, his basement) nodded.

Several minutes of silence followed while the four boys rubbed their heads and considered my questionable band member status.

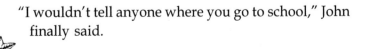

"I wouldn't tell anyone where you go to school," John finally said.

"Just as long as you don't wear fucking cowboy boots," Jude added, "I fucking hate those things."

"Traci wouldn't wear cowboy boots," Jeff smiled, "she's not a cowgirl, she's a pansy."

"Like you," one of the other boys, Scott, coughed.

"Fuck you."

At the time that exchange meant little to me.

Thankfully, I had no intention of ever buying anything as ugly as cowboy boots, and was accepted. My heart felt like a little squeaky red valentine being opened up for the first time.

Jude gave me an awkward pat on the shoulder, "Can we order before we play? I'm starved."

"Traci, you want mushrooms?"

Thank heaven for boys.

That evening, at the dinner table, sans Bradley, my father considered my new adventure with the zest of someone mulling over an old piece of gum.

"A band?" He raised an eyebrow.

"I think it's wonderful," my mother said.

"Yeah," I tried not to look too enthused.

"What's the name again?"

"Cover."

"At least it's not Fuck Your Mother," my dad noted "Or Kill Your Parents."

"That's funny Dad, because the first song on the album is called Fuck Your Parents."

"Must be psychic," my father mumbled.

"Why is the band called Covered?"

"It's *Co-ver*, like, covering other people's songs."

"Oh," my mother smiled hopefully, "is that legal?"

"Just make sure it doesn't get in the way of school next year," Dad warned.

"It won't."

"I say that because I want you to try to be a little

conservative and practical when it comes to your decisions from now on, O.K.?"

My parents were still a little miffed about me throwing out half my closet.

"Clothes don't just grow on trees you know."

"No, they grow in malls."

Of course, the clothes I had purchased, with all my savings, to replace them, had been the icing on the cake.

"You look like a tie-dyed homeless person," my father droned when I came home in a bright red smock lined with daisies.

"I'm not even wearing tie-dye, so be quiet."

"Why do you kids today have to look like you're from the circus?" my mother huffed. "Why can't you just talk out your feelings of isolation instead of expressing them with your clothing?"

Rolling around in a puddle of my new duds spread out over my bed, I felt the keen sensation I could now describe as happy. To this day, that Kensington smell of other peoples' old stuff still makes me smile.

Debut

1:45 p.m.

"No."

"Sure?"

"No, You have it."

It's time to divvy up the last couple bites. My father and I judiciously separate our favorite dishes and vacuum the remaining tidbits. The Yamotos are nothing if not democratic. When we were little, we used measuring cups and a ruler to serve cake and ice cream.

"Oh now," my grandmother would say, patting my brother on the head, "there's enough for everybody, don't you worry."

"If there's enough for everybody," I'd chip in, "There's enough for everyone to have the *same*."

The same.

Nature, for all appearances, is not so democratic.

Bad timing and bad jokes run in my family.

It was a Thursday in September, a perfect afternoon for sitting on the front steps, sun on my face and a light pre-autumn breeze blowing the long red feathers pinned to my twin ponytails at the top of my head. Three days before school, only hours before I was scheduled to drop by the auditorium, along with the rest of my classmates, to pick up my textbooks for the next year. My first day back to school since, you know, *the accident*. Jeff sat next to me, removing and replacing the sequins on my new t-shirt to spell out:

**KISS ME
I'VE BEEN
AWAY**

It used to read:

KISS ME
I'M CRAZY

But my mother stopped me at the door with her arms folded over her chest and a pained look on her face.

"There is no way in hell you're leaving this house dressed like that!"

"Mothering is an angry art."

We compromised and I went upstairs and changed out of my red satin King Henry IV bloomers and into a floor-length skirt Jeff made out of the curtains that used to hang in his grand-mother's room. Over the summer I had discovered that Jeff was a demon with a needle and thread. Too lazy to purchase fabric, he had used up every scrap of material he could find in both our houses. He made me a pair of shorts out of old bathroom towels. I was the only person who would wear Jeff's creations.

"The feathers stay."

"Then the shirt goes."

"Fine."

"Fine."

Communication had become key in the Yamoto household since opting to invest in several rounds of family therapy. Family coun-sell-ing. Mom's idea. Dad's money. My problems.

Bradley, who returned from Young Entrepreneurs in late August with a girlfriend and an airtight business plan to build and sell small CD clocks, was the only one spared.

I spent most of family therapy balled up in Dr. Rosen's plush armchairs trying to massage the knots out of my stomach.

"How do you feel Traci?" Dr. Rosen asked.

"Traci, get your feet off the chair," my mother whispered.

"I feel nauseous."

There was nothing therapeutic in watching my mother cry over old problems and my father stare at the ceiling. My mother insisted she had the right to cry, "You almost died!"

My father insisted he had nothing to say.

Dr. Rosen's puppet body had exaggerated limbs that hung off either side of his chair and practically scraped the floor when he told my parents that my self-mutilation was clearly a sign of a lack of identity.

"You cut because you have no respect for yourself," he said. "Find some way to respect yourself."

"I respect myself," I said. "I'm not going to cut myself anymore."

Four weeks later, at the Swiss Chalet across the street from Dr. Rosen's office, my father and I struck a deal. I would stop cutting myself and we would stop family therapy. Dad wrote up a contract on the Swiss Chalet placemat and I signed it.

My mother continued to see Dr. Rosen on her own every Thursday, while I practiced my singing.

"Doctor Rosen says we should encourage you to test the limits of your environment," she said, several days before school was to begin, "So long as you don't repeat old bad habits."

"That means you can go back to school," my father said.

"I knew that," I hissed, slamming the door behind me on my way to Jeff's, "Crazy doesn't mean stupid."

Back to school.

The master plan was to get on and off the school grounds in the time it would take Jeff to eat his Happy Meal on the side walk outside the school gates.

"I'd go with you," he said, sucking down a fry coated in ketchup, "but I'm allergic to ivy and Protestantism."

From the gateway I could see the steps to the auditorium teeming with excited students. It was everyone's big day, the first day back at school after summer break, the penultimate date on every girl's social calendar, right next to the prom. At my school, where a navy blue and red uniform was status quo for most of the year, there was no better way to make a statement than with clothes on the first day of school. Kate Nelson did it in Grade Five when she wore the first ROOTS t-shirt and multi-layered socks to school, prompting Mrs. Stout, the history teacher, to remark that she "looked cheap."

Kate Sumners did it in Grade Eight when she was the first person to dye blonde streaks into her brown hair. Mrs. Stout said it was time to retire.

I'm sure Mrs. Stout must have done a little roll in her grave that fall when my sequined army boots hit the floor of the auditorium. For half a second the room stood still. A hundred heads turned ever so slightly to take in my outfit. Needless to say, I was the only one not wearing shorts.

Quietly, with my eyes focused on the far wall in front of me, I made my way through the well-tanned crowd to the tables where our books sat waiting. As girls ran across the room to welcome their friends back to school, I focused on the covers of my textbooks, tracing the pink atoms on my science text as I waited in line to sign for them.

"Hey," said Mlle. Lacroix, who taught French, the only subject I was allowed to drop that year, "the cover of the history text-book matches your feathers."

"Yeah."

Kate McDougall, one of the girls who had come to visit me at my house after the hospital smirked, "Nice feathers."

"Thanks."

"Feeling better?" she asked.

. "Sure."

At the cash-out table, two girls from my math class pointed at me, one leaning to the other, whispering in her ear.

"Hey, Mademoiselle, you have to sign out your books!"

I scribbled a hasty signature on my student account sheet and beat a quick exit out the side door.

Sequins and feathers, I decided, were a lousy defense against teenage girls.

On my way out of the school, the religious studies teacher caught up to me and threw her arms around me. Her hair smelled of Pert Plus shampoo and her arms felt like two solid iron locks wrapping themselves around my body.

"Do you feel alright?" she asked. Her eyes were runny with tears.

"No sweat," I said, "I'm fine. Gotta go."

"We should talk," she whispered.

Two steps away a circle of girls in matching grey shorts and v-neck white tops stared.

"Hey! Traci!"

One stepped forward and pointed at my sweater.

"You want a kiss?" she said.

"Yeah," I answered, pointing at the rug in front of me, "The line starts here."

Happy People
Don't Make History

1:53 p.m.

Lately, whenever I see my father it's because I have to sign something. Today is no exception. I'm here to sign papers that will allow him to put my college fund money into a series of investments.

It's a fancy way of saying I'll get the money when I grow up and become more responsible, roughly ten or twenty years from now.

I have a strange relationship with this money, which I've never actually seen or talked about. It doesn't even really feel like my money, since it was left to me by my father's parents. They received it from the government as part of a program compensating Japanese-Canadians for the way they were treated during World War Two. A strange reward for the part my family played in Canadian History.

I never really knew either of my father's parents; both died before I was four years old. I have a picture of me sitting with them on the beach in Florida.

My mother always said I look a lot like my Yamoto grandfather, we have the same round face, the same eyes.

"He was a survivor, too," my mother once told me.

Compensated for our endurance.

There's something incredibly liberating about having everyone in school avoid you because you're crazy. At least when they avoid you, it means you don't have to try and make friends anymore.

On the first day of school my guidance counselor, Mrs. Hopkins, pulled me into her peach-coloured office to talk about the rest of the year.

The walls were decorated with pictures of sunsets.

"It's extremely important to the school," she said, "that you feel very comfortable here. We want you to know that we care about you and want you to be happy." Mrs. Hopkins eye-balled me a little here and pulled a stack of sheets from her desk. "I see you've decided on a pretty heavy course load."

"I want to graduate early. Skip Grade Thirteen."

"Do you really think that's a viable option?"

I let a wide grin spread over my face. "Crazy doesn't mean stupid," I repeated.

"No one said you were crazy," said Mrs. Hopkins. "Are you still in therapy dear?" She suddenly added in a lower voice.

"Not anymore."

"Oh. Well, if you feel better, that's good then."

"Mrs. Hopkins?"

"Yes dear."

"Would it be possible for me to skip religious studies this year?"

Mrs. Hopkins paused.

"I really think I'd feel more comfortable that way," I noted, "I mean, I'd rather not go into why."

"Of course."

I was tempted to push to skip Physics as well but decided against it. All I really wanted was to avoid the hugs.

For the rest of the school year, despite my prized B+ average, my every thought was consumed with music. Jeff, who thought very little of school, or my B+ average, was teaching me to read music in the back room of the Pizza Hut where he worked. When I wasn't practicing I was usually sitting with Jeff among barrels of secret sauce in the back of the Hut. Jeff hated Pizza Hut, one of many stops on his long train ride of useless jobs, and was usually not working. He was probably the only Hut employee who kept a stash of nail polish in the back room. Jeff liked to rotate his nails from blue to black. I had more of a penchant for red and pink.

"I used to do that too," Jeff said, gesturing at the insides of my exposed arms, which, under the neon lights, looked red and white with scars.

"Really?"

"When I was younger and really depressed. Before I came out and stuff."

"Came out as gay?"

"Bi."

Looking down at the scars I realized how long it had been since I had cut.

"Do you still do it?" Jeff asked.

"Not since the hospital, really, I'm too scared."

"Yeah."

"It's weird, because ever since the hospital no one talks to me at school. Because, like, people see the cuts, I used to hide them, now I don't, anyway, I think it reminds them that I'm sick or something. Like now they see the scars and they think 'Ooo, she's crazy' You know? But I don't really mind so much, because it's like now, even though I don't cut, the scars have meaning. Like they remind me. Does that make sense?"

"Yeah," Jeff paused and blew lightly on his nails, "I remember when I first saw your scars, at your house this summer. Something about your scars that day. Made me think, happy people don't make history. I read that somewhere. If you think about it, most of the world's famous people had shitty childhoods. Some of the funniest comedians used to be really depressed. Some still are. Happy people don't make history. When I was a kid, and I used to hide in the garage and play the guitar, I used to think that all the time. It was like my mantra."

"You should write a song: 'Happy people don't make history!'"

"Some day I'll make some dough off all my misery."

"Too bad we only do covers."

Jeff smiled. "You know what you need? You need a tattoo."

"You think so? You think it would help with my would-be rock star image?"

"Like you're a rock star?! As if! Rock stars don't go and see *Truth or Dare* a million times."

I crossed my arms and frowned. Jeff went all of once with me to see Madonna's *Truth or Dare* and he wouldn't let it drop. I liked the movie, O.K?

Jeff smiled. "Outside of giving you rock and roll cred, I think getting a tattoo is nice as kind of a rite of passage. Marks your evolution. First she cut for pain, then she cut for *art*."

"Very deep. What should I get?"

"What do you want?"

I closed my eyes and tried to think of something. Up until then the only tattoos I had ever seen were the hearts and anchors on the men who used to swim at the beach.

"Wings," I finally said.

"Wings." Jeff smiled. "You want to fly away somewhere?"

"Promise you won't repeat this."

"Sure."

"It's like how I feel when I'm singing. Like I'm an angel. Like I'm flying."

"You watch too much TV and listen to too much pop music. All those Christmas specials are frying your brain."

"Maybe. But at least I can fly."

"Wings. I like it."

On my way home, however, while listening to my father's favorite album, I had a revelation that would delay my acquisition of wings.

M-I-N-E

1:56 p.m.

The bathroom is calm and I take time to sit with the echo and the tiles in my little cubicle. Whenever I'm nervous I have a tendency to feel my tattoos. Tattoos are deceptively tactile, raised like Braille on the skin's surface. Unlike feeling my scars, feeling my tattoos gives me a sense of power. I am the mistress of my domain.

I have six. A vine crawls down each of my arms. A solar stem rests on the knot of my spine. A string of bumble bees runs up my back. Around my left wrist, purple and blue lettering. My favorites are still my first two. My angel wings, grey and white, stretching from my shoulder blades to the edge of each shoulder, and my beetle, square in the center of my chest.

Jeff, because he was the only person I knew who could supply me with fake I.D., was the only person I have ever let come with me to get a tattoo. It was on my seventeenth birthday and my first tattoo was a large black beetle which has been sleeping on my chest ever since.

Alex, the tattooist, the ivory-looking bald man who also ran the shop, stood and smiled as I entered the studio.

"Tamara Chong?" he asked, looking down at my fake I.D. then squinting at me.

It's a blessing that to most people all Asians look alike.

"That's me."

"You ready for your beetle?"

"Yep."

"Hop in the chair then."

My black boots clicked against the black tiles as I walked over to the chair in the back room and sat down. Jeff stood in the corner, running his finger over the steel counters.

"Spotless."

Everything smelled cleaned and polished, a mix of new car smell and the smell of hospital linen. I could feel a little buzzing in my chest as I breathed. Nerves.

"Nerves."

Jeff smiled and sat in the tiny chair near the door, fingers drumming on his knees. Cautious and a little shy, I quietly slipped off my blouse. My chest, which was practically the only place I hadn't cut, glowed white, a blank sheet of paper. Alex wiped my skin with a disinfectant that made my chest feel like it had been pounded by a snowball.

"Right here?" he asked, gesturing with the stencil of the beetle that hovered over my chest.

"Here," I said, and circled the spot above my bra in the center of my chest.

The stencil, when the paper was removed, was a delicate outline of my beetle in purple, a little like ballpoint pen ink. The tiny, empty eyes of the beetle stared up at my chin.

Laying his tools out on a small metal tray, Alex launched into his pre-tattoo speech.

"You'll hear the gun buzz then you'll feel the first sting, right? O.K. It feels a little like a burn, which everyone reacts to differently. The only thing I ask for, aside from money, is that you don't move. Tell me if you need to stretch or breathe, or anything else. Otherwise don't move. At all. O.K?"

I nodded, biting my lip a little and focusing my gaze on my chest. Alex leaned forward, elbows digging into my stomach. I could hear his heartbeat. The tattoo gun began to buzz. Guided by Alex's hand, it hovered over my chest, then, carefully, lowered and pressed into the surface of my skin. Tiny raindrops of black appeared where the needle connected with my flesh. Every once in a while Alex would sit up and give the emerging tattoo a wipe with a cloth.

In a moment of silence, while Alex changed ink, Jeff leaned forward.

"What does it feel like? Does it feel like a cat scratch?"

"You've gotten a tattoo before."

"I know but I want to know what it feels like to you."

"Like a thousand needles piercing my flesh. Like a dozen bees doing a tango on my chest."

As I sat in the chair, the slow, sharp burn spread across the surface of my skin. I tried to let my body and brain relax, focus on the one point of pain emanating from my chest. Instead of something printing on my skin, it felt like something was burrowing out from beneath the surface. Something about the buzz of a tattoo gun rang a particular note in my body, something familiar, as pain combined with the exciting awareness of transformation.

I, Tamara Chong, would quickly become what Alex later referred to as an ink fiend.

"Buzz," hummed Jeff.

"I'm trying to concentrate."

When it was finished, my chest was a mess of black and red. Alex took a fingerful of Vaseline and smeared it across the tattoo. The whole thing glistened. I felt like a huge hole had been ripped open in me. I found my reflection in the mirror and stared for a long time, trying to see inside.

"Come on. You're done like dinner. Let's go."

My head swimming in endorphins, Jeff wrapped me in my coat and guided me outside. A fistful of winter slapped me in the face. Large snowflakes zoomed through the tall buildings like miniature flying saucers.

"My chest feels like a brick and my feet feel like feathers," I murmured, weaving a bit as we pushed our way to Jarvis and College. "I'm a little light-headed."

"Come here," Jeff said.

Standing with my chest bandaged on the corner of Jarvis and College, I let a boy kiss me, for the first time. Jeff's lips were deceptively soft, and he cupped my head in his hands tenderly in a way that made me feel safe.

"This is so corny," I said, when Jeff had pulled away.

"Yeah, I know. It was like, oh wow, a moment. I'm such a sucker for moments I couldn't help myself. Plus you're, like, all flushed. It's kind of endearing."

"Yeah. Well, thanks, I mean, for the kiss."

I walked Jeff over to his boyfriend's house. Love in the nineties is strange.

My mother hit the roof.

"Oh God!" She screamed, as she descended into my room with my laundry just in time to see me removing the bandage.

As in Oh God, what have I done to deserve a daughter who would willingly punch a giant hole in her chest? As in, Traci, what in God's name have you done this time?

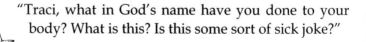

"Traci, what in God's name have you done to your body? What is this? Is this some sort of sick joke?"

If I had been the punching type I would have punched her. I sat crouched on the bed like a tigress protecting her lair.

"Get *out*!"

My mother stormed upstairs. Voices were soon rising and falling. I could hear my mother stomping on the floor in her slippers.

My father, who descended the stairs a minute later, took a more direct approach.

"Who paid for that?"

"Jeff," I hissed.

"Jeff. Really. Then Jeff can pay to have it removed."

"Ha! Are you fucking serious?"

My mother stood beside my father, arms folded across her chest. "You are not walking around for the rest of your life with a huge black blot on your chest."

"First of all, it's a beetle and I like it. Second of all, you can all just fuck off because there's no way you're making me get rid of it."

"Traci!"

They say the first time you actually tell your parents to fuck off is a momentous occasion. My body had become a giant cannon. The giant pearl, festering in the tissues of my gut for so many years, fired out a heavy black cannon ball.

"THERE IS NO WAY YOU ARE COMING NEAR THIS BODY. DO YOU UNDERSTAND? THIS IS MINE!" I screamed, pounding the flesh of my arm, *"YOU HEAR ME? MINE! THIS IS ME, THIS IS WHO I AM AND IF YOU DON'T LIKE IT YOU CAN FUCK OFF."*

"O.K., let's not get dramatic." My father's head was pulsing.

"Thanks Dad. Thanks for dismissing this as dramatic."

"Traci." My mother's voice cut with the delicacy of a dull steak knife.

"Shut up, Mom. Just shut up."

"I beg your pardon?"

Why not let it all out? "You know what kills me? What really kills me? For years I cut my body in pieces and no one in this house notices until I land myself in the hospital. Now, I get a tattoo and suddenly everyone's all in my face. Everyone's pissed off. Why? Because I've finally taken control of my body? Decided that my body is mine? Is that what's so fucking threatening to you?"

"Traci," my mom's voice was barely a whisper, "that's not fair."

"Nothing's fair! Is having your mother in a mental hospital fair? Is being crazy fair?"

"You think this makes things any better? This is better for you? Looking ridiculous?" My father's head looked like it was about to combust.

"At least," my lungs felt heavy and sore, "at least I'm beginning to find out who I am."

"You're a girl who gets tattoos. Terrific. You should be so proud."

"If that's all you can see, then that's who I am."

Lying on my bed, judging the tender soreness of my chest, I thought about it. A girl who gets tattoos. It was an identity I was entirely comfortable with.

I am the girl with the beetle on her chest. I am the girl with the beetle on her chest.

And the wings on her back?

That night, my mother tip-toed into my room and sat on the bed.

"Do you hate us?" she whispered.

"No," I sighed.

"Are you angry?"

Sitting up and rubbing my eyes, I shook my head.

"Then why are you doing this to yourself?"

"Because I have to be me."

I guess it was kind of a lame explanation. In the dark my mother looked small and undefined, a lump of expectation and disappointment. I could hear her breathing, waiting for me to say something else, something better. I was seventeen, what did she expect? An explanation of my complex inner workings?

Maybe if I had stayed in therapy.

"And what is *you*?" my mother asked.

"Not you." I answered, and collapsed back into my sheets.

My next tattoo, when the beetle had healed three months later, was the word M I N E in blue and purple lettering, around my wrist.

"At least you can cover that one with a watch."

My father grumbled.

"Did you read it?" I asked.

"Mine."

"You know what it means?"

"It means you paid for it?"

"Forget it, Dad. Forget it."

Come As You Are

2:05 p.m.

When the bill comes my father lets the tray sit between us for a while. Finally I bend over and grab it, read the final total and smile.

"You know, I could actually afford this. I mean, it would just be this, for a very long time, and we'd have to steal some dishes..."

My father grabs the bill and digs into his pocket for his wallet.

"So, are you making any money?"

"I am. I work a couple jobs on the side. The music is an expense right now but..."

"But soon it will be, what, a source of income?"

The waiter, in his stiff white uniform, raises an eyebrow.

"I was *going* to say that it's an *expense* but I really *love it*."

Every time I get on stage, I feel like I'm glowing. Like I only let my very best of myself on stage, the rest I leave in a bag on the floor. My little Kodak moment. Even when the people in the audience are chucking beer caps at the speakers, I feel untouchable. It's been like that since the beginning.

The very first time we performed it was for a queer anarchist open stage.

RESIST!
featuring:
Glory Hole
Susan Leech
The Flaming Queers
Jeff Striker and the Torpedos
Cover

I was the only one wearing pink go-go boots. A real accomplishment. I got kisses from all the drag queens and a dyke in a tux. We were the last act. Scott had too many beers and threw up on some guy's bike outside the club. Jeff broke up with his boyfriend, who got us the gig, and spent the whole night sulking in the bathroom.

It was great.

On stage, as the lights came up and formed a halo of warmth around me, I was calm. My insides, tense and ready, relaxed. Breathe. During rehearsal I had actually forgotten to breathe and nearly fainted. This time I was bent on respiration.

"Ready?" Scott whispered.

Ready. Holding the mike with one hand, I waited patiently for Jeff's opening chords. In my nervousness, the chords seemed muted, as if coming from the bottom of the ocean. I almost forgot to sing.

"Come, as you are,
have you heard
I'm all you want me to be,
I'm your friend, to the end,
like an old memory."

To this day I am not sure if I was singing the correct words. Jeff said it hardly mattered, although, in the wake of Cobain's death, we did, to our credit, remove the song from our set until we looked up the lyrics.

Singing is the purest thing I'd ever done. For the first few moments I couldn't even open my eyes, for fear my voice would cut out and fade away. Slowly, though, as my voice took flight, I dared to look out over the black sea of audience. All I could see was light, light and the microphone. My hands shook, clutching my skirt, boots twisted in the faded carpeting on stage. I am soooo doing this.

We sang three songs and only had to stop once, when Scott knocked a drum over. I forgot two lines but no one noticed.

"The sure sign of a successful gig," Jeff cheered, pouring the group a beer at the end of the set, "is when they ask you back."

I rule.

After the show, Jeff and I walked to the park and sat on the swings talking all night. Jeff smoked a million cigarettes and I chewed on a movie-sized pack of gummi bears until the roof of my mouth felt raw and splintered.

"You know something," I said, "I think you're, like, my only friend. Is that lame?"

"How many friends are you supposed to have?"

"Six?"

"I think one is O.K. I don't mind being your only friend."

A true friend, I think, is someone who isn't freaked out at the prospect of being your only friend. At five a.m., Jeff got off his swing and knelt in front of me, laying his fuzzy head in my lap. I got off my swing and we sat in the dirt for a long time, kissing, the hard plastic swing pushing on my back.

In the morning, when the sun rose, I noticed the train of picnic benches circling the park, stacked together like circus elephants. Mist rose from the ground. Jeff and I walked home.

My mother was sitting in the breakfast room having coffee when I arrived.

"Doesn't look like you spent the night at Jeff's house," she murmured into her coffee cup.

"We went for a little jog."

"A jog? In heels?"

"Aren't you going to ask me how it went?" I asked, peeling off my sweater.

"How did it go?"

"Good," I said, "and I kissed him."

I went to my room and fell asleep. It was the nicest sleep a teenager ever had. I dreamed of singing circus elephants.

Misty

2:15 p.m.

Outside, Toronto is dirty and the summer sky is winter grey. Business men and women scuttle past us in a rush to get home. My father and I are islands; he tall and tired, his hand raised to shield his eyes from the white light raining from the sky as we wait for a cab at King and Jarvis. Fifteen minutes away, my hotel room awaits me at the Comfort Inn. Mentally I calculate whether there will be any little gin bottles left in the fridge. If not, it's down to the bar for this little rocker chick.

"Didn't you have something to tell me?" My father's voice is a rude interruption to my visions of soothing alcohol.

"Something to give you." From my purse I withdraw a crumpled flyer. "It's a show. Our show."

"I see."

"It's small. At the Rivoli. The only one we're playing in Toronto before we go on the road."

"On the road, huh? Sounds expensive. You taking the bus or something?"

"Dad, it's not like we're bumming around Europe or anything. It's a road trip. We'll be playing and making money as we go."

Or at least that's the plan.

"Right. Sorry."

Frustrated, I shove my hands into my pockets, feel the smooth comfort of the cigarette pack.

"I really wish you'd come."

"We'll see."

"No, I mean really. I mean I really wish you'd come." And even though my insides are quaking, my voice comes out deadpan, like his. Hard, like I don't care, like I'm some politician making false promises to a nation. What I really need is for Glenn Close to walk by. 'Hey Glenn, could you please use your dramatic talent to impress upon my father my intense desire for him to appear at my perform-ance tonight, thus validating all I have worked for for the past two years.'

"You going to sing that 'Fuck Your Parents' Song?" he asks, as I climb into the cab and remove the pack of cigarettes from my pocket.

Sticking the cigarette in my mouth and leaning out the window, I force a smile. "There never was one."

I sailed through my last year of high school with a B+ average and a handful of girls I sat with at lunch. It was like pushing my way across the length of the pool underwater, my eyes focused on the tiles at the other end. I refused to give my parents any reason to think music was anything but a positive influence. Good marks meant they had no reason to complain. My father gave me grim looks during dinner, and I learned to keep my voice down, saving my screams for the taped microphone in Jeff's basement.

What I remember from my final year of high school is authors, not faces. I remember Margaret Laurence and Thoreau, Robert Frost and Descartes, but I couldn't for the life of me tell you who was class president. My guidance counsellor told me to bring my outside interests to school so I took band, only to find out Band 101 meant learning how to play the oboe. I was a bad oboe player but at least, as Jeff pointed out, I was getting better at reading music. For my final exam I played "Misty," during school prayers. It wasn't exactly like my other moments of glory on stage, but I got a standing ovation.

Two weeks before I graduated the religious education teacher had a nervous breakdown. Everyone looked at me when they announced it in class.

"I guess you've been there, huh," said my homeroom teacher, Mrs. Jerkowitz.

"Not exactly," I said, "but close I imagine."

That was the day I played oboe in prayers. Everyone thought it was a dedication.

It wasn't.

The day I graduated, the sun beat down on the soccer field, melting our white dresses and wilting our lily bouquets. Fortunately, as a "Y," I was at the end of the line, in the shade. The only time being a "Y" was ever a blessing. When they read my name, Jeff, Scott, John and Jude all stood up and clapped. They were all wearing black. They looked ridiculous in a respectable goth-like way.

"God! Who invited the freaks in the back row?" A squinty blonde from chemistry class scoffed, two girls away from me.

"Uh, that would be *me*," I said, standing to receive my ticket to freedom.

For my graduation present I gave myself the wings on my back. As the needle punched it's way through my flesh I closed my eyes and tried to think about my future, using a pseudo-Ouija method of divining my next destination. The image that popped into my head while acquiring this transformative tattoo would tell me where I should go. The smell from the bakery downstairs wafted into the parlor and I could think of nothing but bagels.

"Bagels?" Jeff smiled. "Montreal. Definitely Montreal."

"You know what," I said, "You should come too."

"Oh really, to do what?"

"Sing. Play. Be somewhere other than Toronto."

"Sounds very American Dream-ish."

"Except we're talking Canadian cities."

"Could be interesting."

And you know, I wasn't even thinking romance, though everyone we told, including the rest of the band, assumed that's what our re-location meant.

It was too weird and complicated to explain. I wanted him to go with me, so I asked him to come.

And he did.

My mother was the one who saw me off at the station, the stark lighting of the platform setting the perfect mood for my Cindi Lauper "Time After Time" moment. Jeff, already seated by the window above me, was warming up his Nintendo Game Boy.

"He's not even coming to say good-bye," I said.

"Do you have enough money to take a cab when you get there?" Already shuffling in her purse, Mom bent her head so I wouldn't see her face.

"Yeah. I'm fine. Really."

"He'll call. When you get a phone. I'll call too, but he'll call."

"I know." What is it about saying goodbye that changes everything? I stood on the platform with the woman I had avoided for the entirety of my teenage years. I felt totally calm. Maybe even a little sad. Goodbyes are the best family therapy: I may never see you again, so I guess I love you after all.

It occurred to me to say this at that moment, as my mother coyly slipped a twenty into my bag. Looking at Jeff's face intensely concentrated on his twentieth game of Tetris, I couldn't. All I wanted to do was leave. Get out of Toronto and escape my history, good and bad. So I said goodbye without saying I'm sorry. I said goodbye and, for the first time since I was eight, let my mom put her arms around me and hug me. I hugged her back.

On the train, Jeff smiled and squeezed my hand.

"Sad?" he said, handing me the Game Boy.

"Relieved."

"Relieved and sad?"

"Relieved. And a little sad."

The train pushed forward. I watched Toronto slip out of reach, grey buildings blending into stretches of trees, stretches of houses

I had never seen before. For a while I tried to concentrate on each passing detail, but fatigue eventually won out and I lay back in my chair, content to let the past disappear.

Blackbird

11:42 p.m.

The Rivoli

It's been raining all night, a soft rain more like heat than water when it hit my skin as we walked to the bar after dinner. Inside, the room is crowded, mostly art school kids in matching pants and expensive shoes here for the band playing before us. I spend most of the night in the back room, smoking and running my fingers over the scars on my arm. Back at the hotel I had a little, spontaneous crying jag, locked in the bathroom with my face pressed up against the tile. Blame a combination of no sleep, hormones, and lunch with *Dad*, which left me slightly off-kilter and a little uncomfortable in my skin. Now, three hours later, I'm quiet and calm, glad my face isn't puffy and relieved lunch is over. Grateful that I only have a couple more hours to spend in this city. Sitting on the couch, I can feel Jeff watching me. He knows enough to stay away, then helps with my guitar when it's our turn to take the stage.

"Hi, so, thanks for coming everyone."

Blue light in my eyes. I lean forward on my stool, fingers clutching the mike as I imagine Jeff's fingers plucking at the guitar strings. We play five songs, "Jane Says," by Jane's Addiction, Billy Idol's "Dancing with Myself" and between covers slip in ones Jeff or I wrote. Mine's called "Suburban Confessions," though that may change. Jeff asks for requests, and since it's Toronto, no one has any. We play my request.

"This is my dad's favourite Beatle song. 'Blackbird'. It's really quiet, so be nice and don't throw any bottles until we're done."

I always say it's his favourite, but I'm guessing. When I was little, and all the lights were out except the one in Dad's study, I'd creep up to the door and hear strains of "Blackbird." I thought it was a song about birds who worked nights, like lawyers. Now, I sing it to strangers in bars, lyrics newly confessional, like lines from a secret diary written before I was born. Tonight my mouth feels clumsy, like my tongue is tripping over a string of pearls.

Maybe it's better that I can't see the audience, I'll have to paint the picture for myself tomorrow, sitting on the bus as the early morning blurs by my window, grey to green to blue. My father's stoic frame at one of the sticky tables near the back, by the door, avoiding eye contact with my mother, who promised to come, as he watches me on stage, slightly stooped, singing.

"Thanks. Good night."

While the waitress with the glasses and the sore feet clears the tables and wipes them down with the dirty old washcloth, I sit on the stage, quietly winding the last cord up for packing, half sad, half content. Behind me, I can feel Jeff keeping close watch.

"You O.K.?" he asks, voice comfortably familiar.

"I guess."

"Did he come?"

"Don't know. You go ahead, I'll catch up in a minute."

I have my own guitar now. Hugo, the blue guitar. I'm just learning, so the tune is hesitant under my fingertips when I play, tilting my head to listen to the chords echo inside Hugo's belly and reverberate out into the empty bar.

"I am only waiting
I was always waiting
for this moment ..."

Tomorrow on the bus, I will dream of my dad, sitting in the audience, listening to me sing.

Mariko Tamaki is a writer, performer and co-curator of the *Strange Sisters Cabaret* at Buddies in Bad Times theatre in Toronto. Her acerbic pop-culture pieces have appeared in *Blood & Aphorisms*, *Flux*, *Fireweed's Pop Culture* and *Fat Issues*, and the anthology, *She's Gonna Be*. A web-savvy sex toy sales clerk, Mariko is aka web-cam personality Minxy Mittens on www.drducky.com. Co-founder of the fat activist group Pretty, Porky and Pissed Off, Mariko has appeared on CBC radio's This Morning and Newsworld. Her movie, *Shelf Life*, co-written with Lisa Ayuso, can be seen on www.120seconds.com. *Cover Me* is her first novel.